peg + cat
The Penguin Problem

JENNIFER OXLEY
+ BILLY ARONSON

CANDLEWICK
ENTERTAINMENT

One day Peg and Cat were visiting
the very cool, very cold South Pole.
They had come to make snowmen
and to watch the Animal Winter Games.

1+1=2

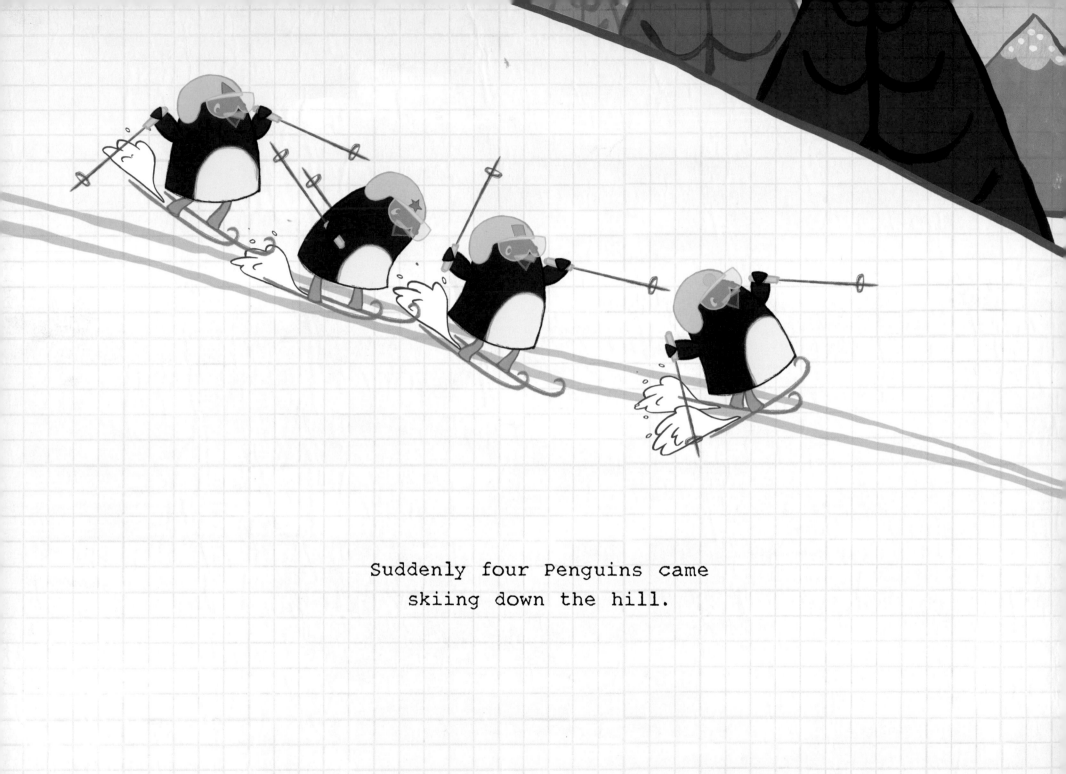

Suddenly four Penguins came
skiing down the hill.

3+1=4

CRASH!

5+1=6

"Sorry!" "Oops!" "My bad!"
said three of the Penguins.

"Please accept our humble apologies!"
said the fourth.

"Snow problem," said Cat,
cracking himself up.
"Get it? Like
'It's no problem'? Ha, ha!"

$6+1=7$

7+1=8

"Are you here to compete in the
Animal Winter Games?" asked Peg.

"Most certainly, yes," said a Penguin.
"But alas, we seem to keep crashing into things."

"Try again!" said Peg.

"Okay!" shouted the Penguins.
"One, two, three, four!
We're the Penguins--
watch us soar!"

With that, they skied off superfast.

The Penguins skied at full speed to the first hurdle.

"GO OVER!"

shouted Peg.

OOF!

OUCH!

The Penguins skied to the next hurdle.

"GO UNDER!"

shouted Peg.

11+1=12

The Penguins skied
toward the flags.
"GO IN BETWEEN!"
shouted Peg.

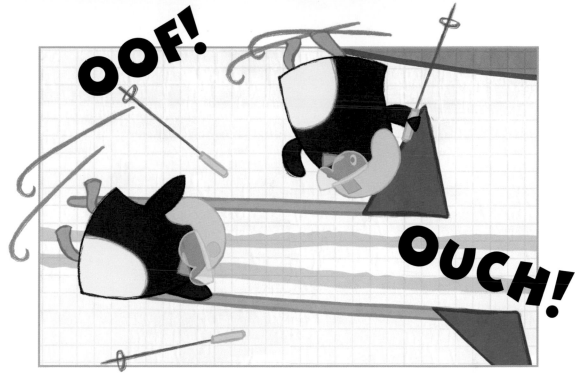

OOF!

OUCH!

"What happened?" asked Peg.

"Well," said a Penguin,
"as it turns out, we don't know what
over, under, and **in between** mean."

The other Penguins nodded.
"Not a clue," said one.

"You'll never win the race if
you don't know **over, under,** and
in between!" said Peg.

**"We've got a BIG
PROBLEM!"**

12+1=13

"Ow," said Cat, who had slipped and fallen toward some arrows.

The Penguins zoomed down the hill again, this time following the arrows.

"Over!" shouted Peg.
The Penguins jumped over.

"Under!" shouted Peg.
The Penguins ducked under.

"In between!"
shouted Peg.
The Penguins skied right
in between the flags.

"They did it!"
yelled Peg.
"PROBLEM SOLVED."

16+1=17

But the problem wasn't solved.
The Penguins were skiing out of control at full speed--
away from the stadium.

"WE'VE GOT A REALLY BIG PROBLEM,"
said Peg. Peg and Cat skied along, shouting:

"Over!"

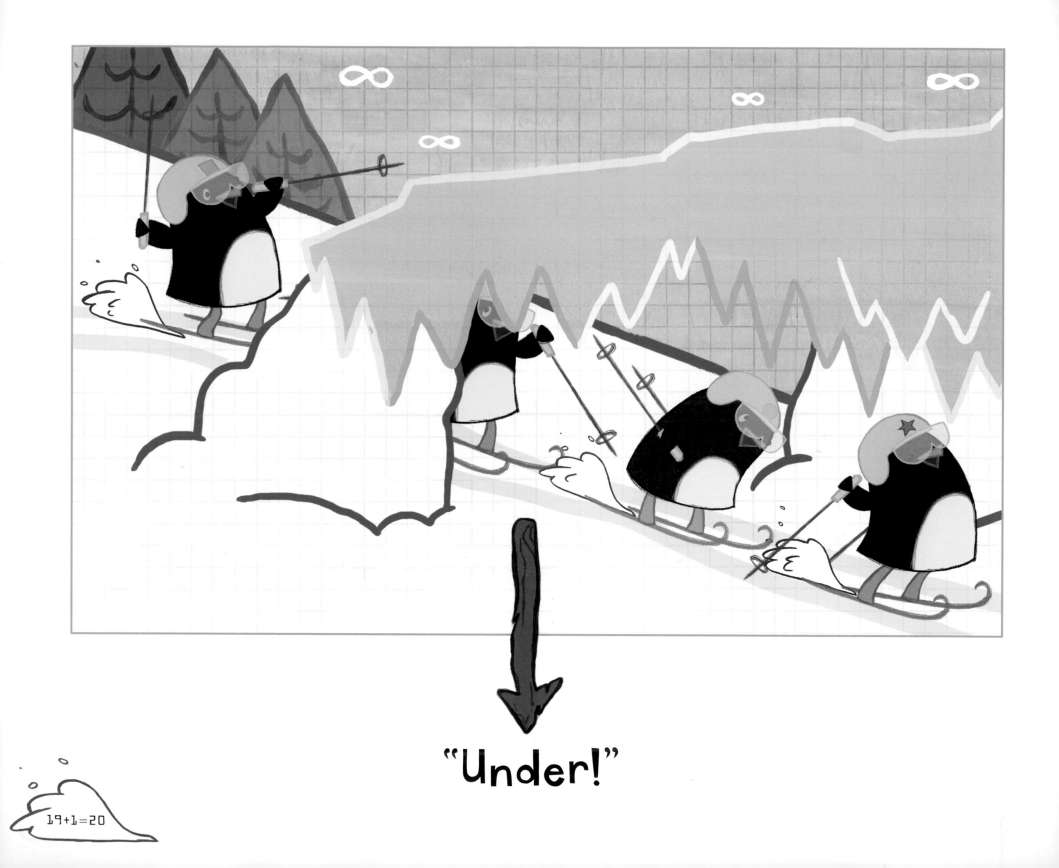

"Under!"

"In between!"

20+1=21

The Penguins skied on and on, up and down the snowy slopes,
over, under, and in between things to keep from crashing.
They smashed through snow piles,
zoomed up a snow ramp and high into the air,
and did amazing midair flips,
before soaring down to . . .

"LAND!" said a Penguin.

21+1=22

"We're not actually on land," said another Penguin.
"We seem to be on a piece of ice
in the middle of the water."

Peg heard Ramone's voice coming from the stadium.
He was announcing the start of the race--
but the Penguins couldn't reach land.

"The Penguins are missing the race!" cried Peg.
"I AM TOTALLY FREAKING OUT!"

Cat held up his paws.

22+1=23

As Peg counted, Cat dropped a big snowball . . .
and rolled it across Peg's ski.

"You amazing Assistant Coach Cat!" said Peg.
"If we use the skis to make a bridge,
the Penguins can go across them!"

25+1=26

In no time, the Penguins were on land and off to the races.

At the stadium,
the race had begun.

The Polar Bears skied
toward the low hurdle.
But instead of going over,
they went **CRASH!**

The Walruses made it
to the second hurdle.
But instead of going under,
they went **CRASH!**

27+1=28

The Squirrels made it to the flags.
But instead of going between,
they went **CRASH!**

Then the Penguins skied up to the
starting gate.

"ONE, TWO, THREE, FOUR!
WE'RE THE PENGUINS --
WATCH US SOAR!"
they chanted.

28+1=29

And soar they did.
The four Penguins skied

OVER

one hurdle,

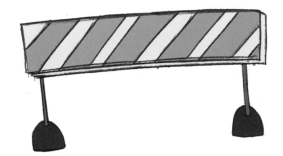

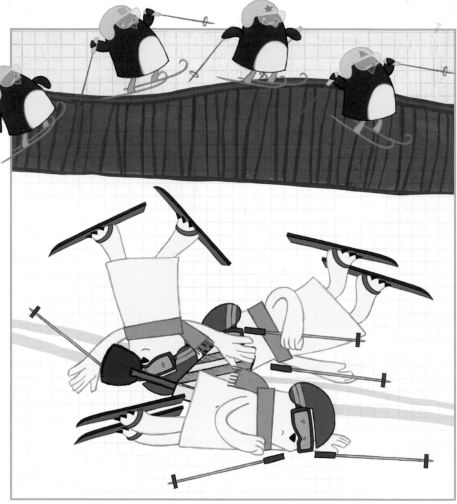

UNDER

another,

29+1=30

IN BETWEEN

the flags,

and all the way to

the finish line!

They were Animal

Games champions!

"WOO-HOO!"

yelled their very proud

coaches, Peg and Cat.

"PROBLEM SOLVED!"

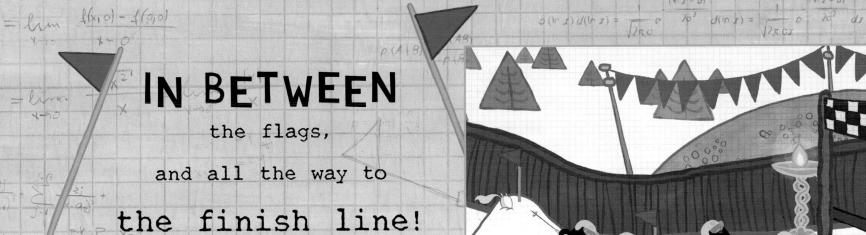

$30+1=31$

This book is based on the TV series *Peg + Cat*.
Peg + Cat is produced by The Fred Rogers Company.
Created by Jennifer Oxley and Billy Aronson.
The Penguin Problem is based on a television script by Qui Nguyen and background art by Erica Kepler.
The PBS KIDS logo is a registered mark of the Public Broadcasting Service and is used with permission.

pbskids.org/peg

First edition 2016

Library of Congress Catalog Card Number pending
ISBN 978-0-7636-9073-1

16 17 18 19 20 21 APS 10 9 8 7 6 5 4 3 2 1

Printed in Humen, Dongguan, China

FSC
MIX
Paper from responsible sources
FSC® C101537
www.fsc.org

This book was typeset in OPTITypewriter.
The illustrations were created digitally.

Candlewick Entertainment
An imprint of Candlewick Press
99 Dover Street
Somerville, Massachusetts 02144

visit us at www.candlewick.com

8

7

6

5

4

3

2

1